Winter Untold

***

Amy Sparling

Winter Untold

***

Amy Sparling

Book 3 in the Summer Unplugged Series

The Summer Unplugged Series

Book 1 - Summer Unplugged
Book 2 - Autumn Unlocked
Book 3 - Winter Untold
Book 4 - Spring Unleashed
Book 5 - The Beginning of Forever
Book 6 - Autumn Adventure
Book 7 - Winter Wonderful
Book 8 - The Girl with my Heart
Book 9 – Autumn Awakening
Book 10 – Winter Whirlwind

The spin-off series:

The Summer Series
Summer Alone
Summer Together
Summer Apart
Summer Forever

Jett's Series:

Believe in Me
Believe in Us
Believe in Forever

CHAPTER 1

Having a moderately famous boyfriend isn't as exciting as I once thought it would be. The good parts outweigh the bad parts by far—like how just last week my boyfriend Jace did a radio interview and gave a shout out to me, his "adorable girlfriend" on air. But lately the bad parts about dating a professional motocross racer are happening more frequently.

I frown as I read the text on my cell phone.

Jace: Um...sorry babe but I have some more slightly bad news.

Slightly being Jace's keyword for when his job has gotten in the way of our relationship again. The first few times he texted me about having bad news, I freaked, thinking he wanted to break up or that something horrible had happened to him. Nope, the first incident was just "bad" in that he had to push our dinner date back two hours thanks to him needing to teach a last-minute motocross lesson.

I let out a long sigh and stare at my phone screen, reading the text again and then scrolling up to read over his previous texts from today. I don't feel like replying right away because my emotions would get to me and I'd just say something rude, or something bitchy and it would ruin both of our moods. Jace Adams is moderately famous after all and by some freaking miracle he chose me to be his girlfriend and I'll be damned if I'm going to screw it up by whining every time his fame gets in the way of seeing me.

But I really want to whine right now.

My head hits my pillow as I stare up at the white ceiling above my bed. Only a few minutes have passed but Jace texts me again.

Jace: Call me when you're free. I love you!

The front door opens and I hear Mom and her new boyfriend teasing each other about who's chicken parmesan recipe is better. It is so weird that Mom has a boyfriend now. I can't remember her ever having a boyfriend, not in my entire seventeen years. But she's happy now so I'm happy for her. Plus her boyfriend takes up all of her free time, leaving more time for me to stay up late on the phone or go out of town to visit my boyfriend. She used to care about these things but now she's too distracted.

Jace answers on the first ring. "Hey there beautiful."

"Don't 'hey there beautiful' me," I say with a smile. "You're about to give me some bad news again, aren't you?"

"Um...have I told you how much I love you lately?"

"Every day."

There's a shuffling on the other end of the line as if he's opening and closing his dresser drawers. "The good news is that I've been asked to help out on Team Yamaha's pit crew, which is one step closer to getting me back into professional motocross," he says. The excitement in his voice radiates through the phone. Jace had to stop racing professionally when he got himself fired for starting a fight with another racer a year ago. Since then he's been teaching motocross lessons at a local Texas motocross track. It sucks for him but it's good for me because professional racers travel all around the country. Teaching lessons allows Jace to stay in Mixon which is just forty-five minutes away from where I live.

"What's the bad news?" I ask even though I don't want to. I'd like to pretend that all news is good news and that the sinking feeling in my stomach is only there because I'm hungry not because my heart is breaking into pieces that each long for my boyfriend.

Jace's voice sounds as sad as I feel. "Well, it's going to put me on the road for six months. I'm still gonna try to see you as much as possible, but the races are every weekend so I don't know how we'll work around your school schedule. But even if I have to see you at night, I'll still come down there."

I'm silent for a moment as once again, I think about how all my problems would be solved if I just dropped out of high school and got my GED. But my mother and boyfriend straight up refuse to let me make that decision. "Okay well, do what you have to do."

"Bay, don't act like I'm choosing this over you. I chose my last job *for* you. So I could stay with you. This opportunity is more than a job. It will affect our future."

I want to snap back that this will only affect his future for the best, not mine. It's not like we're married or anything. But I swallow back my bitchy replies and smile because even though we aren't married, I am still the girlfriend and I plan to stay that way. "It's fine, babe. I get it. I'll survive."

"*We'll* survive," he says. "Don't think I won't miss you like crazy because I will."

I roll my eyes. He doesn't need to sound like such a martyr. I know just as much as he does that travelling around with the rich and famous isn't in any way a form of survival. It's luxury living and he'll get paid for it, too.

Still, it's pretty freaking awesome that I'm dating a guy who hangs out with the rich and famous. Jace steals the thoughts right out of my head. "Plus I'm going to take you with me every chance I get."

"Really?" I ask as I grip the phone tighter.

"Totally. Whatever I'm doing over Christmas break, you'll be with me."

Shit. Speaking of Christmas...my birthday is at the start of December. Jace and I had made plans to hang out at my town's Winter Festival, eat tons of junk food and then have a sleepover in front of the fireplace. He had promised to block off his training schedule for those two days so he could spend them with me. "I guess you won't be able to come to the Winter Festival," I say as I gnaw on my bottom lip. "Or...my birthday."

"I will be there," Jace says, almost too quickly. How could he even know that?"

"You will?" I ask suspiciously.

"Of course, Babe. I won't miss your birthday."

"Promise?"

There's a pause and I feel my heart drop into my stomach. "No. I can't promise. But I will try."

I blink back tears and tell myself to stop being such a baby. Birthdays are just another day. It's not that big of a deal. "I guess a happy surprise is better than a broken promise," I say in an effort to look on the bright side of things. Because even though this situation completely sucks, at least I still have the world's greatest boyfriend.

"I love you, Bayleigh," Jace says. "And that one is a promise."

Chapter 2

An annoying beeping sound wakes me up at six a.m. on Saturday morning. With a groan and a mental threat to murder whoever or whatever is making the noise, I throw off the covers and scramble out of bed to my second floor window.

The sun is barely peeking out above the horizon but it's enough light for me to see the massive side of a rented moving truck. The beeping sound continues as the truck backs into the driveway next door. I guess it's about time that someone moved into that house since it had been vacant for months, but did they have to move in at six in the freaking morning? I don't even wake up this early on school days.

My little brother Bentley crashes into my room in the next instant, screaming my name and jumping on my bed. He stops once he hits my sheets and looks around, confused as to why I'm not under them. When he sees me, he laughs and rushes over to the window and presses his tiny hands to the glass. "Bay, did you see the truck?"

He points to the truck and looks back at me. "It's huge!"

I nod and try to seem enthusiastic for his sake. The kid loves trucks, heavy machinery and anything that makes noise. He also loves waking up at the butt crack of dawn. "It's cool, dude," I tell him in the middle of a yawn.

"We should go downstairs and meet them," he says. "Maybe they have kids my age."

I smile at him. "I don't know about that, it's kind of early." *And I'm dying to get back to sleep.* "Maybe you can go back to bed and Mom can take you to go meet them later today."

Bentley ignores my polite hints to leave my room and grabs my arm. "Maybe they have kids your age too."

"I'm not a kid," I say with mock annoyance as I poke him in the ribcage. "I will be eighteen in two months and that means I'll be an adult."

He gives me a sinister smile. "But that's in two months so you're still a kid now."

My little brother smiles up at me with a sincerity in his eyes and I can't help to smile back. To him, I'm still a kid who still likes kid things and enjoys watching SpongeBob Squarepants with him on the weekends. To him, being a kid is the greatest thing ever. I wish I still had that sweet innocence. I wish I could be content with where I am in life, instead of always wishing I was older and not strapped under the chains of high school and adolescence.

After shooing Bentley back to his room, I crawl back under the sheets in my warm bed and proceed to stare at the ceiling, unable to sleep. Outside is filled with voices and laughter and the sounds of doors opening and boxes moving. It sounds like three or four people just moved in next door.

I hear a high-pitched woman's voice threaten to ground someone if they open another toy box before the rest of the truck has been unloaded. Sounds like Bentley will get his wish of having a new friend to play with. Too bad I don't get my wish of going back to sleep.

6:17 a.m. Me: The neighbors woke me up. Can't sleep. Miss you tons.

6:19 a.m. Jace: Jerks! I miss you more.

The buzzing of Jace's reply makes me jump. I wasn't expecting him to reply so soon. He, like other normal-minded people, likes to sleep in late.

Me: Crap I hope I didn't wake you. I was just texting to vent.

Jace: I'm up. Headed to the airport. You can text me whenever you want babe.

Me: Bring me a magnet!

Jace: Always

The first time he went out of state while we were dating was when he took a trip back home to visit his family in California. He was only there two days, and it wasn't even a special trip but he brought me back this touristy California magnet from the airport gift shop. I loved it so much that he also brought me one from New Mexico and even Houston, despite how we live just a couple hours away from there. Now, I guess it's our thing. Jace gets to travel and I get souvenir magnets.

One day I won't be a little kid anymore. One day I'll get to go with him.

Mom is just as excited as Bentley to learn that a new family moved in next door. After they eavesdropped on them through the cracks in the living room blinds for five minutes, Mom rushes into the kitchen and starts preparing a batch of her famous brownies for them. I don't participate in the window eavesdropping because I am not a weirdo like the rest of my family.

Jace texts me nonstop while he waits at Houston's Hobby Airport for his flight to Anaheim. Mom only makes fun of me twice for my incessant texting, which is a huge improvement from how she used to get pissed off any time Ian, my old boyfriend, so much as sent me one text. But things are way different now. Mom likes Jace. Jace is *so* not like Ian. Plus, my dear old mother has her new boyfriend that she's been texting several times a day so she's just as bad as I am. But she won't admit it, of course.

The doorbell rings right as Mom puts the finishing touches on her plate of brownies that are covered with decorative plastic wrap and for whatever reason, a silver ribbon. Mom is going a little bit out of her way to impress these people. I head over to the front door and stand on my toes to look through the peep hole. Four faces stare back at me, a picture-perfect example of a married couple with two kids.

"Looks like they beat you to it," I tell Mom as I pull open the door. Mom rushes to my side, holding the plate of brownies and introduces herself to our new neighbors. Their names are Melissa and John Williams and they are both dentists. They have a son named Jeff who is exactly Bentley's age which makes everyone way more excited than they should be.

And then there's Chase.

He's a high school senior with sandy blonde hair and exactly the sort of handsome features that would have my best friend Becca throwing herself at him. And, you know, me too, if I didn't have a boyfriend who I was already crazy about.

As it is, I don't give a single crap about him and only waste two seconds of time telling him hello before I excuse myself back to the kitchen and make a glass of orange juice. Mom invites them inside and everyone hangs out around the kitchen island, eating brownies and chatting about the neighborhood.

Chase, with this ripped up jeans and black death metal band t-shirt, won't take his eyes off me. I'm flattered, really, but I also just *so* do not care. It's funny how I felt like no guys noticed me at all when I was single but now that I'm happily in an amazing relationship, a new guy seems to be waiting for me around every corner.

Thinking about Jace makes me miss him as always. My phone hasn't beeped in a while so he's probably boarding some airplane right about how. I look at the screen anyway just in case, but there are no new text messages.

"I think I'm going to head up to my room," I say, interrupting Mom and Melissa's conversation about which of our neighbors are nosy busybodies. "I have uh, homework and stuff I need to do."

Bentley cocks an eyebrow at me, probably wondering why I chose now of all times to do my homework when normally I avoid it until the last minute. But I've said I'm doing homework and I'm sticking to that story because saying the truth: 'I'm missing my boyfriend like crazy and am going to go stalk his Facebook and swoon over his gorgeous photos until he calls me again,' would just make me sound pathetic.

"It was nice meeting you," Melissa says and I smile and return her sentiment as I walk toward the hallway. Chase calls my name and I stop in my tracks.

"Yes?"

He runs a hand through his hair, almost as if he's a little embarrassed to be asking this question. "Would you mind going to school with me on Monday? Show me around and stuff?"

"Uh, sure," I say. It's an innocent enough question and I have no problem showing a new student around the high school. As I head into my room and plop back on my bed, my phone finally does vibrate but it isn't a text from Jace.

It's a Facebook friend request from Chase Williams. That's an innocent gesture, too. No big deal at all.

But something tells me I probably won't be telling Jace about my new neighbor.

Chapter 3

"Having you here is so much better than talking to you on the phone." I wrap my arms around my boyfriend's neck and pull him closer to me as we stand blocking the doorway of my house. It's Sunday afternoon and he just got back into town from Anaheim. When I had asked him how long he gets to stay here, he told me I didn't want to know the answer to that question. He's right; even if he stayed a thousand years it wouldn't be long enough.

"I missed you baby," Jace whispers into my ear. Chills prickle down my body at the feeling of his warm breath on my skin.

"Okay guys, that's enough." Mom taps her foot much louder than necessary from the kitchen. "Jace honey, I'm glad you're in town but you two are going to make me throw up with all the lovey crap." She waves her hand dismissively at us. "Take it to your room."

I smile at Jace and he gives me a sinister grin as his hands slide down my back and squeeze my hips. "I agree with your mom," he tells me. "Let's take this to your room."

We make out for half an hour. There are so many things I want to tell him, like funny stories that happened while he was gone, or random thoughts I got in the middle of the night, but I can't bring myself to pull away from his lips long enough to get any words out. By the way he's hungrily pressing his mouth to mine, I'd say he feels the same. And that's fine with me.

When my lips are numb and my neck hurts from my strained position of hovering over him, I relax and rest my head on his chest. "I miss you more every time I see you."

He sighs. "I know the feeling."

He turns to face me, gripping my cheek in his hand. His eyes trail from my eyes to my lips and back up again. "You look ridiculously beautiful today," he says, ending his compliment with a light kiss on my forehead.

I smile and stare into his bloodshot eyes. Now that I'm paying attention to him up close, it looks like he hasn't slept in days.

"No offence babe but you look like shit."

He laughs. "I'd say I feel like shit, but seeing you makes up for it."

"Were you really busy in Anaheim?" I ask.

He nods. "You have no idea. I spent hours on the track and when I finally finished with lessons, some Team Yamaha high roller would take me to dinner and expect me to drive their drunk ass home at midnight. The best sleep I had all week was on the plane ride here."

I snuggle up closer to him. "I'm sorry. Let's take a nap."

"Sounds like a great idea." Jace stretches out his arms and relaxes on my bed. He winces in pain and then lifts up on his side and shoves his hand in his pocket. "Forgot about this." He hands me a round metal magnet, pink with glitter encased in resin. It says *Hollywood Princess* with a rhinestone crown on top.

"Nice," I tell him as I take the magnet and place it on my nightstand.

Jace closes his eyes and buries his head into my pillow. "I know you're not big on princesses," he mumbles, wrapping his fingers around mine, "But you love glitter and pink..." His voice trails off and becomes a wave of steady breathing as he falls asleep.

It's only seven in the evening and I'm not even a little bit tired but I close my eyes and breathe in the scent of him. I'd rather go to see a movie or get ice cream or just sit around and watch TV, but if the only quality time I can get with him between his business trips involves sleeping, I'll take it.

Jace's iPhone has an alarm ring that could wake the dead. The sound of it, going off at four-fifteen in the morning, startles me out of my dreams. Jace doesn't budge. I shake him a little bit, hoping he'll wake up from his deep sleep and turn off the freaking alarm. The sound blares from his pocket so I reach inside and run my fingers over the phone until it finally shuts off.

Jace yawns. "What's going on?"

"Your alarm just went off."

He opens his eyes, blinking a few times. "It did?"

I roll my eyes and lay back down. "You were sleeping like a freaking zombie. That thing was loud. I bet it woke up the whole house."

He stretches out his arm and wraps it around my shoulders. "Sorry, babe. Guess I was passed out."

I tilt my head up for a kiss and Jace kisses me back but doesn't pursue it much farther than a quick peck on my forehead. Which I guess is fine because I'm sure we both have morning breath. That logic doesn't stop me from getting my feelings a little hurt.

The hurt feelings only intensify when Jace stands up a few minutes later, running his hands over his clothes and then through his hair. He checks the time on his phone and then glances at me, sliding his lips to the side. "Whelp, I'm out of here."

I practically jump off my bed. "What? It's four-thirty in the morning!"

"And I have a six a.m. flight to catch," he says with a frown that looks a little bit forced.

I feel like stomping my feel like a child but I hold back my bratty behavior just enough to say, "Why did you bother coming here if you could only stay a few hours?"

"Because I had a few hours. Why wouldn't I spend them with you?"

Damn him. Always saying the right thing when all I want to do is be mad at him.

His arms slide around my waist a second later, warm and strong as they pull me close. He rests his chin on top of my head and I close my eyes, pretending that just for a few seconds, he's not about to leave me for work again. "I love you, Bayleigh."

"I love you more."

He shakes his head. "You wish."

By the time we tip-toe our way to the front door so as not to wake up my brother or mom, I'm feeling a little less bitter about the whole situation. He came to see me, after all. I should be happy about it. And I am happy about it. I just wish it was a longer stay.

Waking up to one alarm in the morning is annoying, but waking up to a second one just three hours later really sucks. No one should be woken up from a blissful sleep twice in one morning. Especially when the second time you wake up alone and realize it's a school day.

Screw Mondays.

After throwing on the first halfway decent outfit I could find, I head downstairs and root through the pantry for something that even remotely resembles breakfast food. If I leave within five minutes, I'll get to school early enough to hang out with Becca before first period. Monday mornings are gossip catch up mornings. Hell, who am I kidding? Every morning is gossip catch up morning.

I shove a brownie in my mouth, sling my backpack over my shoulder and head out the front door. I'm staring at my cell phone when something soft crashes into me.

Then it talks. "Shit, I'm sorry."

I look up to find myself facing my new neighbor, who's wearing a puffy winter coat that's a little too warm for mild Texas winters. I take a bite out of the brownie and take the rest of it out of my mouth. "Um, hello. What are you doing on my front porch? And why are you dressed like an Antarctic explorer?"

Chase slips his thumbs under the straps of his backpack. "I came to take you to school, and it's cold outside so I'm wearing a jacket." He points to the thin sweater I wear over a t-shirt. "Aren't you cold?"

"Hardly. It'll be hot as hell by noon. Where are you from, anyhow?"

"Missouri. This is the lightest jacket I have."

"Ah," I say, since his overdressing all makes sense now. "Well you won't need that around here. It never gets too cold. It hasn't snowed once in my entire life."

"Good to know," he says. "So your mom suggested that I drive you to school since you were going to show me around anyhow. She said you normally walk when you can't borrow her car."

Ugh. Thanks a lot Mom for blabbing about my entire life to the new neighbors who don't need to know that we're too poor to own more than one family car. It hasn't escaped me that my new neighbors own three vehicles.

Chase holds up the remote on his keychain, points it at a newer model Jeep in the driveway next door and presses a button. The engine roars to life.

"Show off," I mutter.

He laughs. "Remote start is nice in Missouri winters."

I want to tell him that he can take his fancy jacket and expensive vehicle and drive himself to school, but I swallow my annoyance because it is cold outside and catching a ride with a stranger sounds better than walking two miles and freezing my ass off.

The high school secretary is happy to welcome Chase to Lawson High, and she's even happier to volunteer me to be his personal guide through the school, for as long as he should need. Her words, not mine.

I'm a little annoyed at being assigned the babysitter to an eighteen-year-old senior who seems smart enough to navigate the hallways of our small school without someone holding his hand. I guess my new responsibility isn't so bad. He is incredibly hot by Lawson High standards, and I'm his first friend, which means girls will be flocking to me asking me to put in a good word for them.

Like that girl with the anchor tattoo on her arm who hasn't stopped giving me dirty looks in the hallway ever since she discovered that I'm dating Jace Adams. I can't wait to see the look she'll give me when I'm walking with a hot new guy.

Unfortunately, getting his schedule and signing in takes a lot longer than we thought and by the time we leave the office, first period has already started an no one lingers in the hallways to see me walking with my new acquaintance.

"I have yearbook for first period," Chase says, reading over his newly printed class schedule. I hold out my hand to stop him from walking head first into a concrete column in the middle of the hallway.

"I have yearbook too. It's this way."

A grin lights up Chase's face. "Really? How crazy is that?"

"It isn't that crazy. Only seniors can be in the yearbook class and it's a really small class this year so it only makes sense that they'd throw you in it."

"Good point, but I requested this class. I love photography."

I snort. "Sucks for you because yearbook is a lot more than photography."

"Geez, girl, someone woke up on the wrong side of the bed today."

"Something like that," I say, not bothering to tell him that the way I woke up this morning, suddenly blasted awake by Jace's alarm only to have him leave me for the airport, is exactly why I'm in such a crappy mood.

"Luckily other people's sarcasm and general assholery does not affect me, so even though other people might find you hard to be around this morning, I want you to know that I am still in a great mood."

I cock an eyebrow and stop in front of the yearbook classroom. He laughs and pushes open the door. Ugh, that boy really annoys me.

Ms. Jennifer, our yearbook teacher, spends the majority of all classes sitting in the back of the room, huddling over her cell phone, smiling in this creepy sort of way that makes me not want to know who she's texting or what they're texting about. She's in her mid-twenties and the rumor is that she's not even certified to be a teacher but she had a degree in journalism and our school was desperate. All I know is that her apathy makes this the best class ever.

Chase finally leaves me alone in favor of chatting up the yearbook editor, a senior named Eric. I work on my page layouts, choosing to use pictures of students who are my friends even though we're not supposed to be biased. I don't just use pictures of friends though. If someone is a bitch to me, you can bet I'll find the most unflattering photo of them and make sure it gets a spot in the yearbook. That's pretty much why the girl who talked shit about my best friend Becca will be featured on page sixty-four, smiling in the hallway with a shadow casting on her pants exactly in a way that makes it look like she pissed herself.

Whoops! is the caption.

I'm starting to get tired of peeking into my backpack to see if my phone has a new text from Jace. He was in such a rush this morning, I didn't think to ask where he was going or how long the flight would take. Thanks to my forgetfulness, I've now become a phone-checking zombie, desperate for some kind of attention from the guy I love. Seriously. How the hell did people date each other before there was instant digital communication?

"Bayleigh, if you'll stop staring at the phone that you are totally not allowed to have in class, maybe you would be able to answer me?" Ms. Jennifer hovers over my desk, hands on her hips.

"Shit," I say, before dropping the phone back into my backpack and sitting straight in my desk. She's cool and she won't take away my phone, but still, no one likes to be given *the stare* by a teacher. "I'm really sorry, it's a…family thing," I say in a quick scramble to come up with an excuse that will keep me out of trouble.

The look on her face tells me she doesn't believe my made up excuse. "I asked if you will be attending the town's Winter Festival?"

I nod and she smiles and tosses a camera bag on top of my desk. "Awesome. You'll be our second photographer."

"Wait, what?" I put my hand over the bag, wishing I could give it back. "I can't take photos for the yearbook on that night. I'm—I'm busy." Jace flashes across my mind. If he doesn't get out of work then he won't be able to come with me to the festival and technically, I won't be busy. I'd have the whole night free to take as many photos as she wants, but I can't let her know that. And I can't think that way. Even though the chances are slim, I have to believe that Jace will make it for the festival. For my birthday.

"Bayleigh, you are one of my best photographers and if you're already planning on attending then it won't be a problem for you to snap a few photos. She nudges my backpack with her toe, alluding to the cell phone incident a month ago. "Be a team player, and I will be one too."

"Fine," I say with a sigh. "I'll be happy to take some pictures."

As the rest of the class busies themselves with going back to work on the yearbook, I stare at my page layouts and stacks of numbered photographs but I don't work on anything. My mind is far away, worried about Jace and obsessing over this stupid photography thing. Normally it wouldn't be a big deal. I actually like taking photos for the yearbook—it gets me out of all kinds of school work.

But I have a bad feeling about this. I had planned the Winter Festival-slash-my birthday as this magical night. The park is always decorated with Christmas lights and sparkly ribbons, and festive music plays from a live band. The air is cool and the food is amazing and I was going to have picked out the most amazing dress that would make Jace stop in his tracks when he saw me. I don't have the dress yet, but I know I won't be able to find one that makes my boobs look good while there's a stupid five pound camera hanging around my neck.

It's as if all my hope was caught up in this fairytale dream of Jace coming to the festival, and this stupid camera bag just shattered it. It's fate, telling me to stop daydreaming of romance and realize that my boyfriend is too busy for me.

Maybe I should just wear sweatpants to the stupid Winter Festival.

Chapter 4

Becca is waiting for me after school as usual, but this time the look on her face is freaking priceless.

"Becca, this is Chase," I say, swinging a lazy hand between both of them. "He just moved in next door to me and he's giving me a ride home."

"Oh I see how it is," she says with a mock sarcasm. "You're too good to get a ride home with me now, eh?"

"Actually," Chase interrupts with that stupid attractive smile of his, "You're welcome to have her. She's been a bit of a jerk today."

Becca giggles and it's all I can do not to throw up from how much she's flirting right now. Seriously. I mean she's batting her eyes at him and everything. "Oh, you'll have to get used to that," she says, grabbing his arm for good measure. I mean, God forbid he flies away in the wind. "She's always a bit moody."

I guess this sort of behavior is to be expected from her since she and her boyfriend broke up a month ago. Becca pokes at the camera bag slung over my shoulder. "What are you taking pictures of this time?"

"The Winter Festival," I say with a sigh.

"That blows. Are we still going dress shopping?"

I nod and start telling her about the camera strap and dress cleavage dilemma as we walk to the parking lot. Chase clears his throat. "You girls worry about the weirdest things."

My cheeks flush red as I look to my right, having totally forgotten that he was walking with us. "Oh my god, were you listening to our conversation?"

"It's kind of hard not to," he says, smiling at Becca. "Besides, we're all in this together. I need help making sure my camera strap doesn't cover my cleavage, either."

"Shut up," I say. "Wait, what do you mean by camera strap?"

He holds up another camera case with the school's logo on it. "I'm the other photographer. Guess you'll get to show me around the festival as well."

Becca reaches for another slice of pizza while I continue my rant from the safety of my bedroom where freaking Chase can't overhear us. "He is such a stalker! I hate him."

Becca rolls her eyes and pulls off the pepperonis. "You do not hate him. God, you're such a bitch when you miss Jace."

"I know," I say with a laugh. "I just really hate this new guy. I don't need some hot guy moving in next door, trying to be my friend and smiling at me with his stupid perfectly white teeth. I need my boyfriend. Not him."

Becca's eyes bulge out of her head. "Wait, do you like Chase?"

"No, of course not." I swipe all the pepperonis off her plate and eat them. "I only have eyes for Jace. It's just annoying to be around another hot guy when all I want is my own hot guy."

"Okay, I can solve this." Becca holds out her hands like she's about to present to me the best idea ever. "I am your best friend and I am here to save you from crisis like this. So, in an effort to protect you from dealing with Chase, I will simply date him. That way he'll be out of your hair."

"Out of my hair, and into your bed," I say with a snort. "You are such a kind, thoughtful, *selfless* best friend."

"What can I say?" she says, placing her hand across her heart. "I am just *that* good of a friend. I will sacrifice my miserable single existence and take that boy to pound town for you."

I throw a pillow at her as she erupts into laughter. "Please don't ever say the words 'pound town' again."

After dinner and a few more grossly inappropriate sex jokes by Becca, I log onto Facebook to see if anyone has posted anything worthwhile. And by anyone, I mean Jace. And by 'anything worthwhile', I mean anything at all. If the boy had time to update his Facebook but not text me, I'll be a little more than sad.

The good news is that Jace hasn't been online all day. The bad news punches me in the gut.

"Who the hell is this bitch?" The computer monitor warps into weird colors as my finger punches the screen on top of a photo of my boyfriend with some girl at what looks like a rich people party. Jace didn't upload it, he was tagged in it last night by the girl in the picture. There is no caption. But there doesn't need to be one. I can see all I need to know in the picture. Her: beautiful and older than me, with her arm around my boyfriend. Him: gorgeous as always, beer bottle in one hand while the other is around her shoulders. He's smiling and he doesn't look tired at all.

It feels like all the air has been sucked out of me. Becca lets out a low whistle under her breath as she hovers behind me at my desk. "I'll kill her," she whispers in a true best friend fashion.

I shake my head. "It's not her fault. She probably doesn't know he has a girlfriend."

Becca's hand touches my shoulder. "I'm sorry, Bay. Maybe it's not that big of a deal. It's just one photo, it's not like they're sucking face or anything."

I turn off the computer and wipe the tears from my eyes. "I'm sorry but I think I just want to be alone right now."

She nods and gives me the saddest look. "I'm just a call away, okay?" she says before leaving me to wallow in my sorrows.

Jace texts me an hour later, telling me some crap about how he's been trying to call but doesn't get good cell phone signal where he's at. He asked me to reply if I got the message and to tell him what time it is so he knows if he gets it late. Well guess what? I don't reply. I can't find the energy to say anything.

I know Jace loves me but I feel so inadequate. I've always felt that way with him. And then right when I think I get a hold on it—right when I feel like we might be equals—something happens that throws me back into reality where I remember that he is so out of my league.

Jace goes to parties and takes photos with random girls. I go to small town festivals and take photos for a high school yearbook.

A flash of red dives across my darkened ceiling. I look for it again, but see nothing. It must have been my imagination. Even though my phone lights up in a whitish glow, I glance at it just in case. It still has the same three messages Jace has sent me and nothing more.

The red light appears again, this time in a wavy red circle on my ceiling. I recognize it this time; a laser beam. It enters from my bedroom window and swirls around my room before going dark again. Unless someone is trying to kill me, I have a pretty good idea as to why a laser is being directed through my second-story window...but I'm too depressed to yell at him right now.

I walk up to my window from the side, pressing myself against the wall so no one who is looking into my window can see me right away. I peak around the side of my open curtains and see the window of the house next door. Just as I suspected, Chase is the owner of the laser.

He sits on his bed facing the window, watching his TV while he absentmindedly swirls around the laser pointer in his hand. I step in front of my window and pull open the glass, crossing my arms over my chest once the window is open.

He notices me immediately. "Hey, you. What's up? Spying on me?"

I nod. "Yep, you caught me. I totally didn't get up because you made me."

"What?" he says with a coy smile. "I did no such thing."

I roll my eyes and slouch down to sit on my window sill with my side facing him. He cringes. "Don't do that. You're going to fall."

I shrug. "Eh."

"What do you mean by that?" he asks, tilting his head to the side.

"Nothing."

He turns off his TV and walks to his window. We're about ten feet apart now, separated by the ground between our houses and a bunch of awkward hanging in the air. I don't know why I'm sitting here talking to him. I don't even like him. And I don't really want to talk to anyone right now.

He rests his hands on his own windowsill and leans forward, looking at the ground below. "What's so bad in your life right now if you're okay with the idea of falling this far?"

"Yeah, like I'm going to talk about it with *you*."

He shrugs. "I don't see anyone else to talk to."

"Becca was here earlier," I say, changing the subject to the first thing to come to mind. "I think she has a crush on you." *Think* is obviously a lie.

"Oh yeah?" he says, but he doesn't sound as interested as his words imply.

"Well she thinks you're hot. So, I'd say that's interested."

"Hmm." He rubs his forehead. "I can't remember what she looks like."

"Seriously? You saw her earlier today."

He shrugs. "Do me a favor and tell her I'm not interested in dating anyone. I don't want to hurt anyone's feelings, but..." he scratches the back of his neck. "...Yeah."

"Will do, weirdo."

"Why am I a weirdo?"

I don't have to answer this question because my phone bursts into song in the next moment. Without excusing myself, I dive across my room and find an unknown number on my phone's screen. "Hello?" I answer, turning around to see if Chase is still watching me.

"Hey there, Gorgeous."

Chase is still watching, so I give him an apologetic frown and then close my window and curtains. "Hey, Jace."

"I'm calling from my hotel phone since I can't get much cell phone signal. What's up?"

I stare at my nails. "Nothing."

"What's wrong?"

Ugh. I hate being asked what's wrong. Answering the question is never as easy as telling him exactly what's wrong. I wish it was, but it isn't. "I don't know, babe," I say with a sigh. I called him babe instead of *you freaking bastard*, so I guess I'm already starting to forgive and forget this stupid Facebook photo thing.

"I miss you," he says. "Vegas isn't as much fun without you."

"You're in *Vegas*?" My hand balls into a fist.

"I didn't tell you?"

"Of course you didn't tell me!" My voice gets higher but I can't help myself.

"Babe—" Jace tries unsuccessfully to stop my ranting, but I'm on a roll now.

"Why would you bother telling your girlfriend you're going to freaking Las Vegas? The place where what happens there stays there? Because I'd never need to know right?"

"I wasn't keeping it from you," Jace says but I cut him off before he can keep explaining.

"Well guess what, Jace? What happens there won't stay there when girls post it to Facebook."

Chapter 5

Becca speeds through the residential streets from the high school to my house, narrowly missing a dog on the side of the road as she turns onto my street. "Slow the hell down," I tell her as I grip onto the handle on the roof of the passenger side.

"Can't," she says as she slams on the brakes, coming to a stop in front of my house. "I need all the details, now."

I roll my eyes and climb out of the car. All day I had moped around the school, trying to recover from my fight with Jace and how freaking horrible it made me feel. I flat out refused to talk to Becca about it during lunch and also during second and fourth period, the two classes we share together. I had told her it was too much to talk about at school and that I needed to be in the safety of my own bedroom when I share it with her just in case I start to cry.

Judging by the warm pools of tears in the corner of my eyes, I probably will cry.

I guess Becca's desperate need to know all gossip is what made her drive like a NASCAR racer. Although my life was in danger for about ten minutes, at least I didn't have to ride home with Chase. His incessant friendly chatter this morning really drove me insane.

Mom took Bentley to get a haircut, so we're all alone for a while. Becca puts her hands on my shoulders and shoves me away from the refrigerator where I want a snack, pushing me through the kitchen and up the stairs to my bedroom. She drops her cell phone on my bed and crosses her arms over her chest.

"We're home. Talk."

I stare at the floor and tell her about my talk with Jace last night. I tell her about the stupid Facebook photo that he swore was nothing, and I tell her how insanely jealous and pissed off that stupid photo made me. I tell her about Vegas and his many more business trips to come and how I'm just not the girl to handle it. Once I've told her every single detail about last night, and all the subsequent thoughts I've had after it, I sit next to her on the bed and pull my knees up to my chest.

"He wouldn't let me get off the phone until we had made up and were okay again," I say, suppressing a sniffle. "So basically, he thinks I'm not mad at him anymore but I am." I look up at her for the first time since I got in my room. "I'm still mad."

Becca gives me a sad look and I swallow, blinking away tears until my vision is clear again. The fact that I'm still technically not crying is a freaking miracle. Way to go, Bayleigh. You're turning into a cold hearted, take no shit from anyone, bitch.

"You know..." Becca begins, biting her lip while she probably tries to think of something productive to say. *Good luck*, I think. There is nothing productive to say in this situation. I am totally screwed. "I'm not saying you should break up with him," she says, holding out her hands in surrender. "Because I don't want you to break up... I like Jace, I swear. I just... I don't know, Bay. Some relationships aren't meant to last forever."

"What do you mean by that?"

She shrugs. "I believe in fate and I think that if you two are supposed to be together then you'll find a way to make it work. But, you won't have to *force* it to work, you know? It'll just happen."

"Sure feels like forcing it now," I mumble.

"Maybe you should step back and just see what happens. See if you can be happy with him without forcing it."

"I *am* happy with him!" More tears threaten to fall but I force them back. "I want Jace, I don't want anyone else. The problem isn't Jace. The problem is me. I'm stuck in this stupid town, going to this stupid high school. It's not Jace's fault that I can't go with him to these parties. It's mine."

Becca leans her head on my shoulder. "Maybe it's just not the right time. Maybe one day you'll run into Jace at one of those parties and you'll be older and he'll be older and then it will be the perfect time for you to date each other."

"I can't get into those parties without him," I say. I know she's trying to have a productive conversation with me but I can't really pay attention to anything she says because even though she's using many different words, I only hear four: *Break up with Jace.*

"It can work between us, and I want to make it work. I don't want to give up."

"How many teenage relationships actually last?" Her eyes look upward. "I can't think of any of my brother's friends who married the people they dated in high school. Everyone breaks up and moves on and meets other people. This is your first real relationship so the odds are already stacked against you."

"I thought you weren't going to tell me to break up," I snap, kicking her lightly with my shoe. She laughs. "I'm not, I swear. I'm just trying to give you lots of information that will ease the pain in case you do break up."

"It doesn't feel like my first real relationship," I say, twisting my bracelet around my wrist. "It feels like the only relationship that matters. Jace is my soul mate and I want him forever. I'm still so freaking mad about those photos though."

"What was his excuse about that?" She glances toward my computer but I know she's not bitchy enough to make me look at them now. Then again, if Jace has any kind brain, he would have deleted them after I yelled at him last night.

"He said he goes to these big supercross after parties after the races and that he goes with his boss and the Team Yamaha guys. He said he doesn't even remember that girl because apparently—" I make air quotes at the next word, "—*tons* of girls come up to him asking for an autograph or picture. I don't know why he thinks that would make me feel better...tons of girls talking to him every night... but he said he can't just tell them no, so he smiles and takes the picture and then moves on."

Becca shrugs. "That makes sense. I'd be pissed too. That's your man and other girls need to keep their skank hands off him."

"Tell me about it!" My heart twists in pain at the mental image of hot girls lining up to wrap their stupid arms around my boyfriend's waist to take a photo with him. If I were more confident, I'd be proud of him for being so popular. But it's hard to be confident when you're a high school loser stuck in Lawson, Texas.

Becca leans forward on my bed, turning to face me. She has a huge grin on her face, meaning she's already switched topics in her head. "...What is it?" I ask.

"Your new neighbor..." she says with an eyebrow wiggle that makes me want to punch her for being such a dork. "Have you found out any more about him? Is he single?"

"Oh, he's single. He's so single he told me he doesn't want to date anyone."

"What?" she balks with a roll of her eyes. "That's stupid."

"It is stupid. He told me not to even bother trying to set him up with someone."

Her face turns pale. "You didn't tell him I liked him, did you?"

"Nope," I lie. Usually guys are happy to hear that Becca has a crush on them. How was I to know that he'd turn her down? Luckily, he doesn't seem like the kind of asshole to tell her to her face that he doesn't want to date her. I'm sure he'll keep quiet about it so there's no need for me to hurt her feelings.

Becca shakes her head as if shaking off the bad news about Chase's permanent single status. "That boy just doesn't know what he's missing," she says with a sinister smile. "I heard from a little birdy that he's going to Harvey's party on Friday night."

"A little birdy?"

She shrugs. "Maybe it wasn't a bird, maybe I was following behind him in the hallway and I heard him tell Harvey he'd be there. It seemed like they already knew each other which is weird because Chase just moved here."

"So, what are you going to show up and seduce him?" I ask.

"Duh." She punches me in the arm. "And you're going to be my wingman."

"I don't know about that," I say, thinking of high school parties and how completely lame they are compared to the two motocross parties Jace took me to back in the summer. Once you hang out with famous people, high school parties aren't any fun anymore. Plus, Jace won't be there so what's the point?

"Of course you're going!" Becca says, giving me these big eyes as if she knows something I don't. "Hello! Party?"

"So? I don't wanna go."

"It's a party, dumbass. This will be your revenge opportunity. I'll take lots of photos and post them to your Facebook. Maybe get one with you and Chase's fine ass. We'll make Jace jealous."

I laugh. "You are completely evil. Remember when you used to be the shy quiet one and I was the crazy one? What happened to those days?"

"What can I say? You were a bad influence on me." She squishes her bra to adjust her boobs as if to prove her point. "And now we're going to make Jace remember why he chose you in the first place."

Chapter 6

I used to have a love/hate relationship with Facebook. But over the last few days, I've had a whole lot less love and a whole lot more hate for the addicting social network. Three more photos of my boyfriend have popped up on his page, Jace's gorgeous face tagged by some attractive girl I don't know and have never seen before. There are a few girls who occasionally post photos with Jace and it doesn't bother me. Those girls are his cousins, his boss's fifty-year-old wife, and Hana, the girl he works with who is dating his friend.

Everyone else makes me want to punch them in the face. After another ten minutes of going through the newly tagged photos on his Facebook, I sign out and close the computer window. I may not be in control of who posts on his page, but I am in control of how long I'll let myself look at it.

Becca walks in my bedroom, starling me as I spin around in my computer chair.

"Dammit, Bayleigh. You were on Facebook again, weren't you?"

"No..." I say in the world's most guilty-sounding voice.

She puts her hands on her hips and gives me a Mom Look. "Yes you were. I told you to stop looking! Those girls are just excited that they met a famous person. That's all there is to it."

"I know," I say, noticing the lumps of clothing in her arms. "What's that?"

"It's every piece of clothing from my closet that I look even remotely hot in," she says, tossing the pile on top of my bed. "You're going to help me pick out what to wear."

"Oh right. The stupid party." I say it mostly to myself because I'm only just now remembering that I had agreed to go with her to Jackson Harvey's house party tonight. The week really goes by fast when you spend all your time with your head in your hands, thinking about your boyfriend. Jace and I talked a lot more than usual in the last three days. I think he knew I was pretty pissed off and wanted to make up for it as much as he could. As of now, he thinks our relationship is on par, happy as always.

I'm still not so sure. I love the boy with all my heart but I'm not happy with the idea of him having a job that requires partying as part of the job description. He did assure me that it's only for a few months at most, but still. A few months are forever in girl time.

Several outfit changes later, when Becca is as hot as she's going to get in a black V-neck tank top and short shorts despite it being cold outside, we get in her car to go to this stupid party. I've been missing Jace like crazy and he can only call me at night from a hotel phone, so even though the party will be stupid, at least I'll get out of the house. Doing anything is better than sitting around missing him. Becca blasts the heater to warm us up, and I might *accidently* make a comment that she wouldn't be so cold if she'd dress according to the season.

She turns the heater up even higher. "You are no fun anymore. We used to get hot and go to parties together. Now you look like an old housewife."

I furrow my brows and glance down at my outfit. Skinny jeans with black flats and a long sleeve shimmery shirt. There's nothing old about it—it just doesn't allude much sex appeal and that would make the old me very upset. The new me doesn't really care though. "I'm only here for you, Becca. Not for anyone else."

"You could at least look sexy for me," she mutters under her breath. "Wingmen are supposed to be slightly less hot than the person they're wing manning for."

"Wing *woman*, thank you very much." The car slows to a stop and I realize we've arrived at the party much sooner than I expected. A knot forms in my stomach. Do I even remember how to act at a party anymore? It's not like things used to be, back when I was single and came to these things hoping to meet a hot guy and get a phone number or two. And it's definitely not the same as when I go to a party with Jace and get to hold his hand all night, snuggling up against him as the hordes of people stop by to talk with my semi-famous boyfriend.

Now I'm just me—not single and not currently with my boyfriend. Playing wing woman for my best friend who wants to hook up with a guy who doesn't like her. I can do this.

It shouldn't be too hard at all.

Becca leaves the engine running and turns to face me, grabbing my cold hands in her warm ones. "Okay, here's the thing. I might have to tell a few...white lies...tonight. You know, just to make myself look more interesting. As my best friend, I trust that you'll just go along with them and not say anything that would embarrass me. Okay?"

I nod. I know all too well what I've put Becca through in the past—lying about our age to college guys, lying about my curfew, lying about why I didn't have a cell phone—the list could go on forever. Now that the tables are turned, I'm more than happy to do what it takes to make sure all the attention is on her tonight.

"Thanks," Becca says with a smile. "I talked to Chase like four times at school this week so I'm hoping he comes up to talk to me tonight."

My eyes roll around my head in an accidental slip of self-control. I can't help but roll my eyes, and I really wish I could, because Becca gives me a death glare. "Why are you rolling your eyes?"

"I just don't want you to get your hopes up about Chase when he told me very clearly that he doesn't want a girlfriend."

"Right," she says with a roll of her eyes this time. "That hasn't stopped us before, and it won't stop us now."

The party isn't so bad. Usually these things have too many people packed in too small of a house, music blasting so loud you can't hear anything, and very very high chances of getting beer spilled all over your clothes. Harvey's party is the complete opposite of that. His parents' house is a massive two-story McMansion that sits on several acres with a pool in the back yard and a covered patio that's probably bigger than the whole first floor of my house.

The music is kept at a reasonable volume, and I make it all the way from the kitchen, where I grab a Coke instead of a beer, to the back patio without a single person spilling anything on me. Becca asks me to crack open the pull tab on her beer so she doesn't ruin her manicured nails.

We stand near an unoccupied foosball table and I set my drink on it as I open her beer for her. "How many do you think I could drink and still regain my dignity?" she asks as she checks the label on the back of the can. Her face glows pink from the neon bar signs on the walls.

"I don't think the label is going to tell you that," I say, which earns me the stink eye from Becca. "I can usually drink three before I become a total lunatic."

She shrugs. "Three it is. I need to chug this before we run into you-know-who."

"Voldemort?" The male voice is unexpected; Becca and I both jump as Chase walks up from the other side of the foosball table. Chase takes a sip from his drink—also a Coke—and smiles. "I wasn't aware that you-know-who was invited tonight."

Becca bursts into girlish giggles as if she were drunk already. Looks like she got her wish of Chase coming up to talk to her. Unfortunately, he's looking at me.

"When girls say 'you-know-who' they aren't talking about Harry Potter," I say. "They're talking about a guy."

"Oh really?" Chase asks enthusiastically.

Becca gives me a quizzical look, probably wondering if I'm about to rat out her secret. I just shrug. "Duh."

Chase looks at Becca now and she takes a long sip from her beer. "Well, good luck. I hope you-know-who shows up and sweeps you off your feet. Or, you know, whatever girls want guys to do."

"I don't need luck," Becca says with a sudden burst of confidence. "Want to play foosball?"

Chase obliges and I lean against the wall nearest them, finishing my Coke and getting another. Staying sober at a party where nearly everyone else is drinking is a new experience for me. For one, everyone isn't as hilarious as they seem when you're drunk. Mostly everyone just looks like an idiot.

Chase beats Becca for the third time at the game of foosball, but she isn't the least bit upset about it. She calls for a rematch, again, and starts in on her forth beer. Looks like I'll be driving us home tonight.

My phone rings around nine p.m. and I almost miss the sound of Jace's ringtone over the music thumping from the surround sound speakers on the patio. I pull my phone out of my back pocket and realize that I did miss his call—three times.

"Hello?" I answer, knowing I won't be able to hear him over the loud party noise. The decibel level seems to be a lot higher than when we first arrived. "Hold on a sec, I need to get somewhere quiet."

I push my way around groups of people and into a spare bedroom so I can get some privacy. Unlike in the movies, there's no one making out in here. "Jace?" I say into my cell phone, now that I can hear him.

"Hey, sweetheart." His voice sends a warm shiver down my spine. Oh how I've missed his deep voice and his sexy body and his warm, strong hands.

"I miss you," I find myself saying instead of hello.

"I miss you more," he says.

"Impossible!" I laugh. "You're traveling around having all your meals paid for...I'm stuck here in Texas. You can't possibly miss me more than I miss you."

"I don't know about that... it sounded like you were having some fun yourself just now."

"Ugh, if you only knew. I'm at this stupid party with Becca and she's drunk so I get to be her babysitter and watch her try to make out with a guy who has no interest in her."

Jace laughs. "That sounds like Becca."

We talk some more about the party and it amazes me how he doesn't once say anything that would hint to him being jealous that I'm at a party without him. Every other guy I've known would get really pissed if I went to a party alone, but not Jace. He really is freaking amazing. I don't deserve him one bit.

We talk for half an hour and Jace catches me up on the meetings he had today with his new employers. They're offering him a lot of money to stay on board and continue doing training and promo activities for him, with the promise that he will be able to race for them in the future. He's super excited about it and I am too, if only for him.

"You're a little quiet," he says after a while.

"I'm just thinking," I say, leaning my back against the wall in someone else's house. "I'm so happy for you but I'm going to miss you a lot."

"It won't be like this forever," he says. "I promise. Oh! Crap, I almost forgot to tell you." His voice gets really excited and my heart skips a beat as I wait to hear what he has to say. "I think there's a ninety percent chance that I'll make it down there for the Winter Festival."

"Really?" I practically break my cell phone with how hard I squeeze it. "I'm so excited!"

"It's not officially official, but it's mostly official."

"OhmygodIloveyousomuch."

Jace laughs. "I love you more."

I hang up the phone feeling as though I'm floating on cloud nine. When I open the door to the empty bedroom and step into the hallway, someone whooshes past me, making me press back into the wall.

"There you are."

I glance around, thinking surely he's talking to someone else. Why would Chase be wondering where I am? He pokes me in the shoulder with his index finger. "I've looked everywhere for you."

The beer on his breath hits me now. Guess he stopped drinking Cokes a while ago. I put on a fake smile. "I was in the last place you looked. What's up? Where's Becca?"

He shrugs and flashes me a smile. "She's making out with some guy. I don't care though. I want to see you."

Alarms go off in mind. This is not good. "I need to find Becca," I hear myself saying. Something flashes in Chase's eyes now, a look of recognition as if he suddenly sobered up enough to realize that he's been hovering in my personal space, making flirty eyes with me. He blinks, and the look is gone. Replaced with a drunken smile again.

"So," he says, poking me in the shoulder again as he takes a step closer to me. We're only inches apart now, close enough for me to nuzzle against his chest if I wanted to. I definitely don't want to. "I think you're cute."

"Um, thanks," I say, still trying to keep my smile, still trying to stay nice for the sake of not making things weird.

"We should hang out."

Becca bursts into the hallway now, her hair all disheveled. She looks positively pissed off. "Bayleigh!" she yells, looking into the living room and then back down the hall, where our eyes meet. "We need to get out of here," she says, stomping down the hallway and grabbing my arm without even glancing at Chase. "Now."

Chapter 7

It's funny how when life gets crazy, the normal mundane things keep going as if nothing happened. Like school on Monday morning. Becca drives me to school, not saying a word about last Friday where she drunkenly made out with some guy only to have her ex-boyfriend stumble onto the scene and punch the poor guy in the face.

In first period yearbook class, Chase walks in just before the bell rings and slides into his chair which is next to mine. He gives me the same nod hello like he does every day, and doesn't mention or even hint to whatever weirdness happened between us last Friday. Everything goes on normally, as if last Friday didn't happen. As if I am the only person who remembers it.

So, despite the craziness, everything is basically normal. Except that when lunch comes and goes, I still haven't gotten any texts from

Jace...but I guess that's normal now, too. I hardly ever hear from him anymore.

I'm checking my cell phone for messages as I walk down the long hallway that leads to the parking lot after school. As expected, there's nothing from my boyfriend.

Someone taps me on the shoulder and I glance over to see Chase giving me a sheepish grin and he falls into step with me. "Hey."

"Hello," I say, turning back to my cell phone.

"Look, I'm sorry about last Friday. I was drunk and an idiot. I don't even remember what I said."

"Then why are you apologizing?" I ask, lifting an eyebrow. I hoped he had forgotten about calling me cute, but he's probably just pretending he did.

"Because the only thing I do remember is the look you gave me in the hallway."

"What kind of look was that?"

"He stares at the ground as he walks. "A look like I'm a fucking asshole. So I want to apologize."

"Ah," I say as the moments of silence grow increasingly awkward. "Well, thanks."

"Winter Festival in one week," he says, hooking his thumbs around his backpack straps. "I think we should go together since you know all about it and I'm still the weirdo out-of-place new guy. I can drive us."

I want to tell him that I can't ride with him because I'll be with my boyfriend. But I can't say the words because then I'd end up jinxing myself and Jace won't be able to make it. Or worse, he'll call and break up with me and then I won't even have a boyfriend for the festival. Luckily, I don't have to say anything at all because Becca smashes into my other shoulder one second later.

"Looks like I don't have to take your ass home today," she says, giving me a silly eyebrow wiggle.

"What do you mean by that?" I ask right as I look up at the parking lot, toward the second row where Becca's car is parked. "Oh, my god..." I murmur as the world's biggest, goofiest grin spreads across my face. I think Becca says something but I don't notice whatever it is. All I can focus on is my boyfriend's big ass truck, parked directly behind her car, and my boyfriend, looking handsome as hell in dark jeans and a black leather jacket, staring straight at me.

I break into a sprint and cross the parking lot, leaving Chase and Becca in my wake. Jace gives me his silly smirk, trying to play it cool when I know he's just as excited as I am. He opens his arms and I dive into them, wrapping my hands tightly around his neck as I feel my feet lift off the ground.

His breath is warm against my neck, a huge contrast to the cold air outside. "I missed you, baby," he says. Chills run down my neck and prickle across my spine.

"I missed you too," I say, or rather, *try* to say. My words are cut off by his kiss—his lips are warm and smell slightly of minty lip balm.

"You two have fun," Becca calls out sarcastically as she taps her foot while waiting at her car door. She can't move until Jace drives his truck out of her way.

"Oh we will," Jace calls back, opening the passenger door for me.

I turn to wave goodbye to Becca, but see Chase instead. "See ya," he says with a small smile, but he isn't fooling me. He had no idea I had a boyfriend.

And I'm an idiot for not realizing that until now.

Chapter 8

Mom and her boyfriend take Bentley to dinner and to see a movie, leaving the house completely empty for a few hours. I pounce on Jace as soon as they leave the house, sliding my fingers up his chest and desperately wanting to leave the living room in favor of my bedroom. Preferably, my bed.

Jace pulls away after a minute of kissing. "I want to finish this, trust me I do, but can we get some food first?"

I frown, drawing my eyebrows together in a puppy face. "Food is more important than making out with me?"

"Never," he says, pulling my forehead to his lips. "I'm just so damn hungry. I've been on a plane all day and unsalted peanuts can only hold me over for so long."

I roll my eyes. "Okay, but I want Italian."

"Pizza?" he asks with a smile.

I grab my purse off the couch. "Duh."

Nick's Pizza has the most amazing giant pizza slices. They really are giant in that you pretty much have to eat them with a knife and fork. One slice is served on a metal plate which is actually just a large pizza pan. Jace always orders two slices and I always order one, which extra marinara sauce because Jace doesn't eat his crusts and I eat them for him.

Having a routine like this really means a lot when our relationship has been less than routine lately. We sit on opposite sides of a booth in the back corner of the bistro. Jace tells me stories about idiots on the plane ride and how he saw two business men fight over an outlet in the airport.

"You sure have a lot to say about the airports," I say, dipping a piece of crust into the marinara sauce. "Funny how you have nothing to say about those crazy parties you go to."

"They aren't crazy," he says, aiming his fork at me. "Plus, you act like partying is my job. It's not, ya know. I spend most of my day covered in sweat and exhaust fumes out on the track."

I want to say something snarky or mean, or comment on the stupid girls at those stupid parties, but I hold off and just try to enjoy the moment with my boyfriend. There's plenty of time to be mad at him when he isn't here.

The way he stares at me now makes me wonder if he's reading my mind.

"I love you," he says.

"I love you," I say back with a mouth full of food.

He smiles as he watches me, finally saying, "It felt like you hated me the last week or so. I don't know if it's the distance or what, but I've been really worried about us for the last few days. Then I get to see you in person and everything feels fine."

I nod. "I kind of feel the same way."

"What do you mean by that?" he asks, leaning in.

"I mean sometimes I kind of hate you when you're not here," I say in a lighthearted but still serious way. He lifts an eyebrow. "Is it because of the parties?" he asks.

I shouldn't even have to justify that dumbass question with an answer, but I do anyway. "Yes."

He reaches across the table and grabs my hands, looking me in the eyes. "I promise I will not attend another after party without you."

"Babe..." I say, glancing at the table. "You don't have to do that. Now I feel bad."

"Don't. You're my girl and I'm going to do what it takes to make you happy."

A weird mix of extreme satisfaction and overwhelming guilt flow into me. His promise to me is definitely what I want, but why do I feel so damned bad about it?

My eyes close as Jace kisses a trail down my neck. We're back at my house and my mom and brother haven't returned yet, so we've left my bedroom door open to hear them when they get back. Jace's lips kiss my collar bone and chills run down my arms. I grab his head and pull it to me in a hug. Making out on the sly with the looming knowledge that the front door will open at any second, ruining our private time, is no fun. Well, it's a little bit fun.

But still. "You're acting weird," I tell him as I draw light circles across his scalp with my nails. He slides his hands around my waist and locks his fingers together behind my back.

"You know me too well," he whispers.

"So what's going on?" I ask, trying not to sound so disappointed. "You're leaving soon, aren't you?"

He sighs. "At midnight."

"Ugh," I groan. "I was hoping you'd at least get to spend the night like last time."

Jace pulls back and adjusts himself on my bed, resting his head against my headboard and pulling me into his lap. "There's some good news though."

I cross my arms defiantly. "How could there possibly be good news?"

"I was thinking you could drive me to the airport then just take my truck home with you. That way you could keep it until I get back next week. No more bumming rides with Becca."

Or Chase, I think. Countless possibilities float across my mind...if I had his truck for a week, I could drive myself to and from school, the mall, the bookstore. Anywhere I wanted. I wouldn't have to beg Mom for her keys or bribe Becca to take me somewhere she doesn't want to go. A whole week of freedom...

"Wait, you're going to be gone a *week*?"

He laughs. "Yeah, but before you figured that out, you looked pretty happy."

"I am," I say with a roll of my eyes. "I'm excited. I can't believe you're trusting me to drive your truck."

His eyebrows narrow. "Well... I trusted you until you said that..."

I give him a playful slap and then immediately regret it because he pins me to the bed and tickles my ribcage in the exactly the most ticklish spot. I lash out in laughter, unable to stop the giggles and squirming. I hate him so much some times. But in the best possible way.

The long, romantic goodbye I had pictured on our drive up to the airport is ruined the moment

Jace and I walk into the terminal. Two women who might be old enough to be his mother come rushing up to him with the typical star-struck face I've come to recognize lately.

Jace slowly lets my hand fall from his as he goes in to return the hug the first woman throws at him without even asking. Talk about an invasion of his personal space. Plus her perfume smells like she went to a cheap perfume kiosk and sampled every bottle.

I stand idly by, hands clasped together in front of my body, waiting for my boyfriend to finish small talking with these women. He autographs things for them—an iPod case and a dirt bike magazine—and takes a dozen pictures because the second woman keeps looking at each one and determining that it's not good enough for Facebook, so can he please pose with her again? Ugh.

Ugh, ugh, ugh. So much ugh. I hate people who love my boyfriend.

When they finally leave, Jace pulls me close to him and sways gently as we stand at the furthest part that I'm allowed to walk without having a plane ticket myself. I press close against his chest, closing my eyes to block out everything else. I smell him and feel him and listen to his heartbeat which is much faster than usual. I hate these goodbyes. The ones that feel like it will take an eternity to see him again.

I don't pull away until Jace reaches into his pocket and pulls out his truck keys. "Here ya go. Take care of her. I left a credit card in the glove box if you need gas money," he says. "Or, you know... pizza money."

I smile, feeling entirely more important than I am, and take the keys. I may be losing Jace for a week, but at least I get a piece of him to take home with me. Or, a piece of him that will take *me* home, rather.

Chapter 9

I get home around midnight, the same time Jace's plane is probably leaving. It takes a lot of effort to climb out of his truck and go inside, but it's not because I'm tired. This truck smells like him. That's why I don't want to leave it. In fact, I don't even want to sit in the driver's seat out of fear that my shampoo or laundry detergent will rub off and wear away his scent. But then I realize that a normal, sane person would not be thinking these things, so I suck it up and pull myself out of his truck, determined not to be as crazy as I want to be.

The moment my head hits my pillow, a red laser beam dashes across my ceiling. I crawl out of bed and walk over to my window, kneeling to the floor. I push open the glass and lift an eyebrow at Chase, who is also sitting near his window. "What could you possibly want at midnight on a school night?" I ask.

"Sorry. I saw your light on just a minute ago when I couldn't sleep. Figured you couldn't sleep, too."

"I just got home, actually." I yawn, despite myself.

Chase looks like he hasn't slept in a while. His white undershirt glows in the light of the moon. He rubs the back of his neck. "I just wanted to say that I didn't know you had a boyfriend until today. So I'd like to apologize for how I've acted around you. If I had known earlier, I wouldn't have... well you know."

"No, I don't know," I say, leaning forward. "It's fine, Chase, you haven't done anything wrong."

"I know I came on to you at that party. I don't remember doing it, but I know I did. I had a huge crush on you and I started drinking so I'd get the courage to go say hello, but by the time I found you I was a little *too* drunk."

I smile, remembering that night. I'm grateful he doesn't remember it, but all he did was call me cute. He was sort of a total gentleman while drunk, which is saying something. Most guys aren't. "It's fine," I tell him.

"So how long have you been dating Jace Adams?" he asks.

"A few months. How did you know his name?"

He snorts. "Because he's kind of famous, duh. He seems like a great guy, Bayleigh. I'm really happy for you. "

"He is," I say. My eyes drift off as I think about him and how much I miss him.

"Is everything okay?" Chase asks, pulling me back to reality.

I shrug. And then I do something really embarrassing. I tell him about the Facebook photos. And Jace's long business trips. And my jealousy. The Winter Festival and my birthday and how I'm terrified that he won't be able to come. And, well, everything else.

Chase leans against his window frame as he listens to me recount everything that's happened between Jace and me lately and how it's making me wonder if I'm good enough to date someone with such a busy schedule.

Finally, when I've said all I can say and am feeling more depressed than ever, I stop talking and glance up at him. He frowns. "Bayleigh you need a hug. But my arms aren't long enough to hug you from here so, just listen."

The seriousness of his voice gets my attention. He continues, "The Facebook photo thing does suck, but I believe him and you should do. Girls do that shit...they take photos of hot guys and plaster it all over their Facebook so they can look important. They aren't important and Jace does not care about them, I promise."

"How can you promise me that? You don't know."

He nods. "Yeah, I do know. You are absolutely beautiful and one of the most fun girls I've ever been around. Jace knows that, too. He knows he's the luckiest guy around to have you and he sure as hell won't throw that away on some skank at a party that he'll never see again. He left his truck with you. That's a pretty big deal."

I feel warmth rushing to my cheeks and I'm glad it's too dark outside for him to see me blushing. "Thanks, Chase. I needed that."

"No problem. I'm great at reassuring hot girls that their boyfriend loves them," he says with a boatload of sarcasm. "You should get to bed. You have school tomorrow."

I laugh. "*You* should get to bed! You also have school tomorrow!"

Chase stands and puts his hands on either side of the window pane, preparing to push it closed and block me off for the rest of the night. "So yeah… sorry for all the flirting with you."

"Is that what you were doing? Flirting?"

He rolls his eyes and slides the window closed, apparently thinking I was being sarcastic. I wasn't though, and now I'm wondering if he's the sarcastic one. He sure seemed apologetic for it though, so maybe he was. Another thought occurs to me as I watch his light turn off and I slide my own window closed.

Maybe he doesn't have a thing against girlfriends. Maybe he just didn't want Becca as his girlfriend.

Chapter 10

Becca holds a clothes hanger up to her body while the golden dress that hangs from it presses against her. She turns to the full length mirror on the wall of the dress store and stares at herself. Her lip curls in disgust.

"What's wrong?" I reach out and touch the satin fabric, trailing my hand down the skirt. "It looks good and it's a great color for your skin tone."

"That's the problem." She grabs the paper price tag affixed to the shoulder and swings it around in my direction. "It's three hundred dollars. I can't afford this."

"Whoa," I say, gingerly taking the hanger from her hand and placing it back on the rack. "I only have a hundred dollars to spend and that has to cover shoes too."

Becca looks longingly at the golden dress. "I have eighty-six. But I probably have shoes at home that could go with a dress."

We look around the store, a family-owned formal wear outlet that occupies an old Wal-Mart, and find a section of dresses for a much lower price. I'm bummed that the more beautiful dresses are out of my price range, but I keep reminding myself (and Becca) that this isn't prom. It's just the Winter Festival and it's not a real formal event but people like to get really dressed up for it.

Back at home, Bentley already has his little black tux laid out on his desk in preparation of the festival. I'm still trying to find something that's hot *and* cheap. The only thing that would be worse than not finding the perfect dress would be finding it and then attending the festival without Jace.

As if on cue, my phone lights up with a new text message.

Jace: I miss you baby.

Me: I miss you more. Guess what I'm doing?

Jace: Um...watching that show about zombies?

Me: I'm shopping for a new dress.

Jace: What for?

Becca gives me a concerned look but I turn away and pretend to look at ugly pink dresses at the rack closest to me. My phone feels heavy in my hand as I debate what I should text back. I can't believe he doesn't remember why I would be shopping for a dress. I guess he had no intention of coming back here to go to the festival with me. Maybe he's even forgotten that it will also be my birthday.

Me: If you can't remember why then I guess I don't need to keep shopping.

Five minutes go by. I slump into an uncomfortable chair outside of the fitting rooms and watch Becca parade by in three different golden dresses, all within her price range and all pretty awful compared to the expensive one. I still don't have a reply from Jace and I've never been so freaking hurt in my life. This is my boyfriend. The guy I am completely crazy about. The guy I thought was completely crazy about me.

I almost jump out of the chair when my phone buzzes.

Jace: I don't care what you wear to the festival, I just want to be there with you.

Normally that would be sweet. But right now I'm just not having it.

Me: Have you figured out if you'll be in town or not?

Jace: Not yet.

Another hour passes and we're still at the dress store, only at least now I'm not watching Becca try on dresses in her price range. I'm trying on shoes just for the hell of it. Having given up on looking at the dresses, I've ventured over to the countless racks of discount shoes, ranging from boring black flats to six-inch stiletto clear plastic heels with rhinestones all over them.

Who needs to waste money on a stupid dress anyway? Not me. Why would I want to look beautiful and dressed up at a place where I won't even have a date? The digital camera that's property of Lawson High School will be my date, and it doesn't care what I look like.

Later, after having convinced Becca that I'm totally fine and my quietness is only because my head hurts and not because of anything bothering me, I begin doing what I've gotten really good at lately: lying on the bed, staring at the ceiling. It seems to be the only pastime I can find the energy to do now that the large rock of depression has formed in my throat and settled in the center of my chest.

Is my relationship over?

Why is that all I can think about?

I glance out the window but Chase isn't at his house. That means I won't be able to casually walk past my window a million times, hoping to "accidentally" see him. It seems strange that I'd rather talk to Chase about my problems than my own best friend, but lately everything is strange. Plus maybe I just need some guy wisdom.

My phone hasn't rung all afternoon, and texting Jace in the dress shop is the last I've heard of him. I remember back when he worked at Mixon Motocross Park just forty-five minutes away, he would talk to me all day long. A lot of guys aren't into constant texting or phone calls, and I can understand why. Normally, I wasn't into that either. But Jace and I were talkers and texters and we loved staying in contact with each other all day long. From the Good Mornings to the Good Nights, I spent an entire summer and fall counting on Jace to be there for me whenever I needed him, and even when I didn't need him.

Now he's like a distant memory, an old relative who only calls on Christmas or birthdays. Okay, maybe it isn't that dramatic. And he still finds a way to talk to me at least once a day, so our relationship isn't bad, by any means. A lot of guys don't like talking all day. It just sucks because Jace didn't used to be one of those guys. Now he is.

I know I shouldn't do it, but I log into Facebook anyhow. My heart beats rapidly inside my chest as I log in and look at my newsfeed. I don't know why I get so nervous every time I check the stupid social network...it's not like I'm doing anything wrong. It's not like I'm hacking into *his* account.

(Although it'd be a lie if I said I never thought about it.)

I type in Jace's name and go his profile. A sharp pain pierces through my heart when I see the newest update to his page. Yet another girl, this time much younger and very beautiful, has uploaded a photo of herself and Jace. They're very close, leaning in next to each other as she extends out her arm to take the picture herself. The caption says, 'I met my favorite racer today! I'm so star struck, lol!'

My heart aches as I stare at my boyfriend's face in the photo. He's smiling, albeit a little bit forced. I know that logically he doesn't like her and he probably doesn't even remember her name. Just because he took a photo with her doesn't mean he's going to leave me for her. I know that. I do.

But it doesn't make it hurt any less.

I miss my boyfriend and I need him to be with me.

With a sigh, I take out my phone and break the silent treatment I've been giving him since I was at the dress store.

Me: I miss you and I need you with me.

No better text than the truth, I guess.

His reply is instant.

Jace: I miss you more and I need you even more than that.

The pain in my chest doesn't ever seem to go away.

Me: Then come homeeee!!!
Jace: Soon, baby. I promise.

Chapter 11

When the bell rings after school on Friday, I don't rush out of class toward the parking lot like everyone else. I grab my backpack and head down the hallway toward yearbook class. With all my depression over Jace and the fact that he's not going to make it to the festival tomorrow, my school work has been slacking severely. And the one thing that can't be put off any longer are my yearbook pages. I can let down myself with bad grades in every other subject, but I owe it to the entire school to get this yearbook finished on time.

Focusing on something other than Jace should be healthy for me. I've got to pull myself out of this funk and get back on track with life. Just because he can't make it for the festival or my birthday doesn't mean the whole world stops spinning. If anything, it just spins faster.

When I make it to the yearbook room, someone is already in there, sitting at a desk in the back corner. It isn't the teacher, but I hadn't expected to see her for a while anyway. She always heads outside after school for a quick smoke. The student in the classroom, already busy at work on a double page spread, is Chase.

I toss my bag on the floor next to his and sit at the table next to him. "You're behind too, eh? I have like five overdue pages that I'm supposed to send to the publisher by Monday."

Chase shakes his head, and lifts up the papers he's working on which look very familiar. "No, you have four overdue pages. I just finished this one."

"Wow." I take the oversized paper and look over the layout of the images, the perfectly spaced captions and perfect little additions to the pages I had started. "Thank you." No one at school has ever done anything so nice for me before.

He slides the paper across the table and reaches for the next one. "It's no problem. You've been struggling all week so I thought I'd help you out."

I take a stack of photos and pull off the paperclip that's holding them together. It's a collection of students from the football team, all wearing Halloween costumes. "How did you know I've been struggling?"

His head tilts to the right and he lifts an eyebrow. "How could I not know? You've been shuffling to class with the saddest look on your face all week. I didn't see you get any work done…you just sat there staring off into space."

"Actually, I was staring at the bulletin board," I say, pointing to my left where a worn out bulletin board fills half of the wall. Did you know there are three push pins with glitter on them? The rest are all clear."

Chase clicks his pen and begins writing on a notebook. "Fascinating."

I try to think of something to say to break up the silence. "Are you ready for the Winter Festival?"

He shrugs. "I guess. I heard the food is pretty good."

"I wish I didn't have to go." I run my finger over the border of one of the edited yearbook pages. "The food is good, but that's about the only good thing this year."

"Boyfriend can't make it?"

I shake my head but he's focusing on his work so he doesn't see it. "He's too busy with work stuff, I guess."

"Sorry to hear that."

We work in silence for a while, finishing up two more double page spreads. I want to tell him that he can leave any time he wants to because I don't really need his help anymore. The work is pretty much done. But I can't bring myself to say it because I like the company. What I do say catches me by surprise. "I saw more photos on his Facebook."

Chase pulls off a photo and rearranges it on the paper. "Of the same girl?" He doesn't have to ask what I'm talking about—he knows.

I shake my head. "No, but it still hurts."

He waits a beat before responding. "Did you talk to him about it?"

"Not this time. I've kind of just been ignoring him."

He nudges me with his shoulder as he applies a glue stick to the back of a photograph. "Uh, yeah, that's not going to solve anything."

"Trust me, I know." With a deep breath, I let it out slowly and look down at the fake wooden texture of the table. Chase always says what I need to hear, but I never want to hear it.

Chase clicks his pen closed and sets it on the table with precision, like it's important and what he has to say now is also important. I look up at him. He crosses his arms over his chest and looks back at me.

"You know what your problem is?"

I stare straight ahead, not answering. Because how the hell am I supposed to respond to a question like that?

He continues, just as I knew he would. "Your problem is that you're living for someone else. You need to live for you."

"What does that even mean?" I ask.

"You obsess over your boyfriend. You cater your everyday—your every choice—to this guy. You are incapable of being happy without him. That isn't healthy, Bayleigh." He points his finger at me, letting it poke me in the chest very lightly. "You are the only person you should live for. Boyfriends are just a bonus. Make yourself happy first. Learn to have fun by yourself."

I roll my eyes. "What are you, some kind of psychologist?"

"No, I'm just a seventeen-year-old with a logical head on my shoulders."

"Ugh," I groan. "You can be really annoying."

He looks over and gives me a smirk. I punch him in the arm. "But, thanks for the advice."

Chapter 12

I've been wake for thirty minutes on Saturday morning, which means I've spent a whopping twenty-nine of them trying to follow Chase's advice and 'live for myself'. The first sixty seconds of the day were a total waste because I laid in bed staring at my cell phone, wishing I had something new from him. Then I pulled my shit together, got dressed and went for a run around the neighborhood. The Bayleigh who lived for Jace didn't go for runs...she just sat around hopelessly waiting to hear from her boyfriend.

The new Bayleigh, the one who lives for herself, doesn't do that. Nope, she runs and frees her mind from all thoughts of boys. Okay, maybe I'm still trying to figure that part out. After my run, I took a quick shower and went to the kitchen to make some breakfast. Mom isn't awake yet and Bentley seems to have already made himself breakfast, if the drops of milk and bits of cereal on the counter are any indication.

I eat my own bowl of cereal and watch TV, purposely choosing a girly makeup-themed reality show that I know Jace can't stand. I'm doing a really great job of living for myself. I'm actually proud of my progress, even though it's been only less than an hour. I'm not even thinking too much about the Winter Festival tonight and how I'll be going without a date. Yep, I'm a changed girl now. I live for myself. Then my phone lets out the chime that signals an incoming text message, and all bets are off.

I catapult off the couch, barely setting down my cereal bowl without spilling it everywhere. My phone is upstairs where I left it this morning, thinking I didn't need the temptation of seeing it constantly because then I'd want to check it constantly. However, now I'm pissed that I have to run across the living room, up a flight of stairs, down the hall and into my room to get it. It could just be anyone else texting me but I have a really good feeling it's Jace.

It is a message from Jace, but it's not a text...it's a picture. My foot taps anxiously on the floor as I wait for the thing to download. The signal in my house is awful and it takes a good two minutes for the message to finally show up. When it does, I'm confused. I was imagining it would be a picture of him, but it's a picture of a piece of paper on top of a tacky hotel bed sheet. I click the picture and zoom in, trying to make sense of the rectangular piece of paper.

The first thing I see is a tiny black picture of an airplane in the top corner of the paper. Then I see Jace's name. It's a boarding pass. Chills whoosh over me as I read the words on my phone screen. It's a plane ticket. To Houston.

And it lands in three hours.

I'm so excited I might throw up. Another text comes in a few seconds later, this time it loads instantly.

Jace: Hope you have your dress ready!

Tears of happiness had pooled in the corners of my eyes at the first message, but the second one sends me into full freak-out mode. I never bought a dress! I have nothing to wear tonight! Thanks to my morning run, my hair isn't even washed. Oh god oh god oh god.

When I emerge out of the shower a little while later, my only thoughts are concentrated on getting to the mall ASAP so I can find a dress and then begging Becca to help me with my hair and makeup. My mother has other plans.

"Happy birthday!" I hear in a chorus of cheers from my mom and little brother as I walk downstairs in search of my hair dryer. On the kitchen island sits a cookie cake with my name written on it in icing. It's circled with what is probably eighteen candles, though I don't bother to count.

"Aw, guys thank you," I say as I untwine the towel out of my hair. As usual, Mom has her camera ready to snap a photo of me. At least no one else is here (like Jace) to witness my embarrassment at being pictured next to a cake wearing pajamas and having soaking wet hair.

Even though all I want to do is run around and freak out about Jace and the Winter Festival, I squash as much of my anxious freak out as I can, and try to enjoy some family time with them. Bentley gives me a present that he wrapped in Christmas paper, saying Christmas is close anyway and it's just wrapping paper so it doesn't really matter.

I open it to find a collection of photo frames made out of Legos, all including funny pictures of us throughout our lives together. The adorableness of his gift has me completely forgetting about Jace. I hug him and promise to cherish the frames forever.

Mom says she needs to get her present for me next and walks to the hall closet. Curious, I watch her pull out a black garment bag that has a pink bow and a card attached to the hanger. I pull off the card first. It's a gift certificate to Nina's Beauty

Salon—good for a manicure and hair styling...for two.

"Why is it for who people?" I ask, barely able to contain my excitement. I could totally use this today to help me get dressed for the festival.

Mom smiles. "Well it was Becca's idea. She knew you were worried about the festival tonight, so I figured I'd get both of you girls set up for the evening. You have an appointment in thirty minutes."

I dive across the couch and wrap my arms around her. "Oh my god, Mom, you're the best!" She hugs me back and says simply, "Duh."

"I haven't even told you the good news yet," I say, remembering my text from Jace that resulted in my jumping into the shower before telling anyone else about his plane ticket. "Jace is coming home today, just in time for the festival."

She nods. "Oh, I know. So does Becca." She nudges the black garment bag. "Open your other present."

I unzip the bag to reveal a beautiful shimmery blue strapless dress. My mouth falls open. The dress is amazing. It's absolutely perfect. "How did you...?" I begin, unable to find the right words. How did she pick the greatest dress possible?

Mom laughs. "Becca and I bought it out when you stayed late at school. Jace had told her through Facebook that he wanted to surprise you for your birthday and she was afraid that you had given up on the idea of going to the festival."

I am both elated and annoyed that my mom and best friend knew about Jace's surprise visit and didn't tell me. But then again, it wouldn't have been much of a surprise. "Thank you," I say, feeling overly emotional. "I'm going to call Becca."

"She'll be here in a minute," Mom says just as the sound of Becca's car engine roars from our driveway. I hear her door close and I run to the door to greet her, excited for the next few hours of getting all fancied up for what will surely be the greatest Winter Festival in the history of Lawson.

Chapter 13

The timing of our salon appointment means I have to drive to the airport to pick up Jace while wearing a face of makeup and a head of gorgeously-styled hair. It's worth it though, to see the look on his face when he steps out of baggage claim and sees me for the first time.

"Nice pajama pants," he says as he grabs me in a hug that lifts me off the ground. "It really goes with your hair."

"Well I couldn't very well wear a fancy dress to the airport," I say, squeezing my arms around his neck while he spins me in a circle before setting me down. As much as I want to make out in the airport, I also want to get the hell out of here so no random girls recognize him and beg for autographs, ruining our special time together.

Luckily, we make it out of the airport and to the truck, walking hand in hand and with no interference. Jace is excited to see his truck again, claiming that taking taxis everywhere gets really old, really fast.

"I took care of her," I say as I climb into the passenger side. I prefer sitting over here. Because when I'm on this side of the truck, it means Jace is on the other side. And that's exactly where I want him: with me.

Jace plucks a photo of himself off the dash where I had placed it the day after he loaned me his truck for the week. "I can see that," he says, handing me the photo. "You can have this back."

We spend a couple hours at my house, gorging on cookie cake and hanging out with Becca until it's time to go to the festival. Bentley entertains Jace in the living room while Becca and I get dressed in my bedroom.

I admire my pretty new dress in the mirror. "It's beautiful...especially the cleavage part. Too bad I have to wear that stupid camera," I say with a frown.

Becca fastens a pearl earring and joins me in front of the mirror. "Negative. I've already arranged to take the pictures in your place."

"No freaking way," I say. Becca hates yearbook class and she really hates doing anything that promotes school spirit. She shrugs. "Consider it part of your birthday present."

When Jace and I arrive at the Winter Festival, I can't stop smiling from ear to ear. The park is decorated in a bazillion clear lights and the food smells amazing. Everyone is in a great mood and the weather is absolutely perfect. It's not too cold, but still chilly enough to give me an excuse to snuggle up against my boyfriend, who is looking ridiculously hot by the way.

We drink hot chocolate and wave at Becca every time we run into her. She's made it her goal to photograph as many unpopular students as possible in her own way of sticking it to the popular students.

Even though Jace isn't much of a dancer, I'm thrilled when he takes my hand and leads me onto the makeshift dance floor that's usually a basketball court. A band plays Christmas carols under the basketball goal, and spotlights light up and change colors, turning the concrete into a colorful winter wonderland.

Everything is so perfect and yet so disheartening at the same time. All night, I've tried to focus on the good and happy things. I've tried to ignore that hint of sadness that keeps poking its head around the corner, reminding me that tonight will only last a few hours and then life will go back to normal, with Jace in another town and me here missing him.

"So how long are you staying this time?" I feel the disappointment creep into my bones before he can answer. He's probably leaving tonight. Maybe tomorrow morning if I'm lucky.

Instead of answering me right away, he lifts an eyebrow, pretending to be confused. "What do you mean?"

I squeeze his shoulders in frustration. "Don't play dumb with me. You know what I mean. When are you going back on the road to go do fancy famous people stuff?"

He laughs. "Did I forget you tell you?" he asks with a coy smile tugging at his lips. My chest goes cold as I stare into his eyes, wondering what he's keeping from me.

"Tell me what?"

He hesitates, clearly enjoying the thrill of leaving me hanging in the balance. His fingers tighten around my waist and we sway gently to the music. He kisses my forehead and I roll my eyes. "Tell me already!"

"I'm not doing any more fancy famous people stuff," he says.

"What do you mean?" I ask, afraid to get too excited just yet. I'm sure the other shoe will drop soon.

He smiles. "I quit. I'm done with it."

"What?!" I stop dead in the middle of the dance floor. That was his dream, there is no way he quit. "Why did you--?" I begin, stopping when I can't finish my sentence. "You didn't get in trouble again, did you—"

He cuts me off with a shake of his head. "No babe, I didn't get fired. I really did quit. I'm keeping my job at Mixon where I can help train kids to be professional racers. I don't want to be a professional racer anymore...it isn't worth it. Fame isn't worth it."

There's a seriousness in his eyes that tells me he's being sincere. He truly feels that way, and my heart leaps with happiness that his true feelings just happen to align with mine.

"I want to be with you forever," he says, looking around and gesturing to the festivities going on all around us. I'm almost startled by the sight of all the lights and people because being with Jace had made me forgotten that anyone existed besides us. "I want this. I don't want fame."

I can't say anything for a long while. I just bury my head into his chest, close my eyes and sway to the music, getting lost in the wonderful feeling of being in the arms of my love. When I do speak, I say the first thing that comes to mind.

"This is the best birthday present ever."

***

Don't miss the next installment: *Spring Unleashed*

Or listen to the books in Audio book format, read by Disney Channel actress Cheryl Texiera!

Want to get an email when Amy's next book is released? Sign up for her newsletter here: http://eepurl.com/bTmkPX

Don't miss the spin-off series based on Bayleigh's best friend Becca's life! The Summer Series is available now:
Part 1- Summer Alone
Part 2 - Summer Together
Part 3 - Summer Apart
Part 4 - Summer Forever
About the Author

About the Author

Amy Sparling is the author of The Summer Unplugged Series, Ella's Twisted Senior Year, Deadbeat & other awesome books for teens. She lives in Houston, Texas with her family and a super spoiled rotten puppy.

Amy loves getting messages from her readers and responds to every single one! Connect with her on one of the links below.

Connect with Amy online!

Website: www.AmySparling.com
Twitter: twitter.com/Amy_Sparling
Instagram: instagram.com/writeamysparling

Made in the USA
San Bernardino, CA
13 January 2017